What lies at the end of the rainbow? Is there merely a pot of gold, or might there be another sort of treasure — a treasure that may be reached by anyone willing to undertake the journey?

For if you follow the rainbow to its end and look into its shimmering colors, you will find a great oak tree with a door at the base of its trunk.

If you open the door and step inside, you will meet Mrs. Murgatroyd, the wise woman who lives there. In her paint pots she collects all the colors of the rainbow.

And if you take up a paintbrush and picture whatever is in your heart, you will discover a treasure far more valuable than gold.

# Painting the Fire

*Enchanté books are dedicated to the children who inspired them*

Series concept by Ayman Sawaf and Kevin Ryerson
Stories developed from actual case histories by Liz Farrington
Text copyright © 1993 by Enchanté Publishing
Illustrations copyright © 1993 by J. Douglas Moran
MRS. MURGATROYD Character copyright © 1993 by Enchanté
MRS. MURGATROYD is a trademark of Enchanté
Series format and design by Jaclyne Scardova

Enchanté Publishing,
180 Harbor Drive, Sausalito, CA 94965

Printed in Hong Kong

*Library of Congress Cataloging-in-Publication Data*
Farrington, Liz
Painting the fire / story created by Liz Farrington; written by Jonathan Sherwood;
illustrated by J. Douglas Moran. — 1st ed.
    p.    cm.
Summary: With the help of Mrs. Murgatroyd's magical paints, Ryan learns to deal with his
anger and to confront the class bully.
ISBN 1-56844-001-4
[1. Anger – Fiction.   2. Bullies – Fiction.]   I. Sherwood, Jon.    II. Moran, J. Douglas, ill.    III.
Title.
PZ7.F24618Pai                    1993                    [Fic] — dc20                    92-76022

First Edition
10  9  8  7  6  5  4  3  2  1

# Painting the Fire

Story created by Liz Farrington
Written by Jonathan Sherwood
Illustrated by J. Douglas Moran

*Enchanté Publishing*

"**H**ey, Ryan! You need a haircut!" Mark hissed as he yanked Ryan's hair.

"Ow!" Ryan swiveled around in his seat and slapped Mark's hand. Hard.

"Stop it this instant!" said Mrs. Jarvis. "Ryan, that's the third time today." She scrawled his name on the blackboard. "You will sit on the bench during recess. Do you hear?"

"No fair!" cried Ryan. "He pulled my hair!"

"Mark, I hope what Ryan says isn't true. Ryan, you've been hitting and kicking everybody for weeks. I've seen it myself and I've had it. Now kindly keep your hands and your feet to yourself."

"I hate school," Ryan said through his teeth as he pounded his desk. Mrs. Jarvis stared at him until he looked down, then she continued with their lesson on dinosaurs.

*Tyrannosaurus rex,* Ryan said to himself, thinking of Mrs. Jarvis. *And Mark's a Triceratops sticking his horns in my back.*

The bell rang and Ryan jumped. Recess. As his classmates filed out, he shuffled over and slouched on the bench near the door.

Mark walked by, smirked, and stuck out his tongue. Ryan slid his foot out and Mark tripped — spilling right into Brandon, who knocked over Molly Barnes, the smallest girl in the class. She crumpled to the floor like a rag doll, and began to cry.

In a second, Mark was on top of him. They tore into each other, punching and snarling, rolling on the floor. Ryan was skinny and no real match for Mark, but Miss Marlin, the teacher's aide, had to help Mrs. Jarvis pull them apart.

"He stuck his tongue out at me!" Ryan shouted.

"*Hush!*" said Mrs. Jarvis. "I've had it up to here with you."

While Miss Marlin led the class out to the playground, Mrs. Jarvis marched Ryan to the principal's office. She told the secretary about Ryan's misbehavior, glared at Ryan, and stomped out.

The secretary strolled to the door. "Mr. Thompson is in a meeting, Ryan," she said as she stepped outside. "Just sit tight. He'll be with you in a little while."

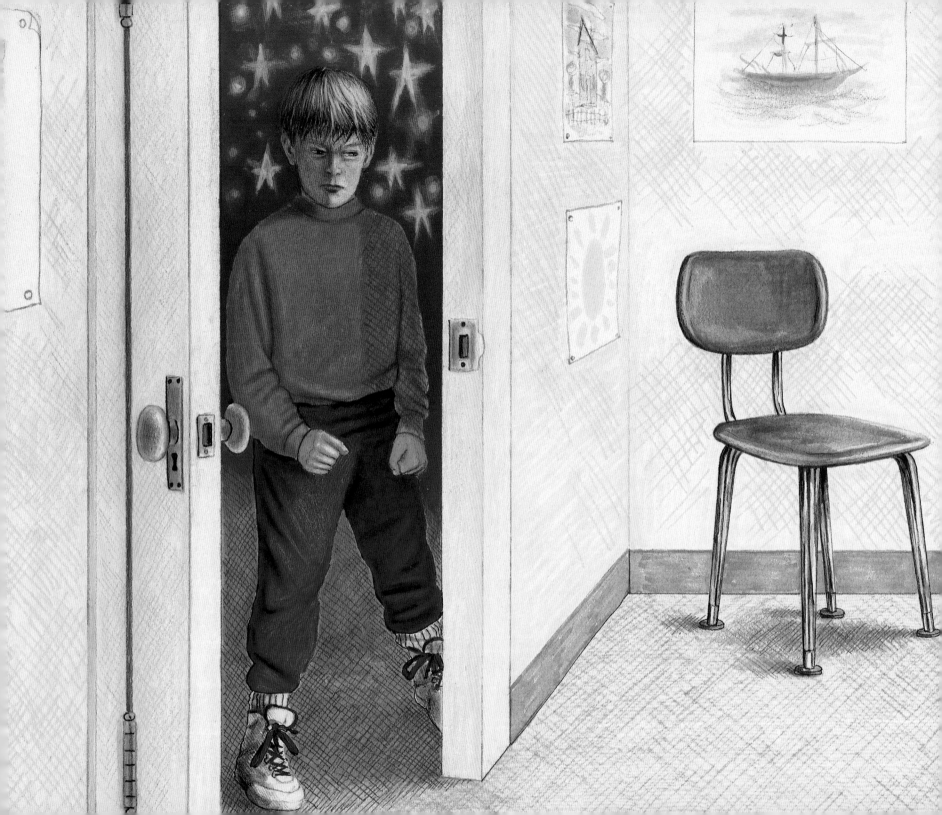

*"Just sit tight,"* Ryan said, mockingly. He felt like breaking something. Fuming, he fidgeted and kicked his heels against the chair legs. *Mark pulls my hair and I get blamed. Sticks his tongue out, but I get sent to the principal's office. Teases me. Just 'cause I daydream a lot. And I'm not so good at sports. He gets to be a captain all the time, but never chooses me for a team. Or if he has to, picks me last. Last! Then makes fun of me.*

Feeling like he'd explode if he kept sitting there, Ryan sprang up and stormed down the hall, pounding his fists against his hips.

"I could *kill* that Mark!" he said to himself. "And Mrs. Jarvis, too. She always takes his side. She never listens to me."

The art room door was open. Ryan peeked in. Nobody. He quickly stepped in, shut the door behind him, and sat down at a table. Trembling, he buried his head in his arms. Tears of frustration stung his eyes.

Suddenly he heard a sound. Ryan looked up anxiously. He knew he wasn't supposed to be there. The art room looked different. It shimmered in the light of a rainbow. An unfamiliar teacher was collecting all the rainbow colors in paint pots. *Where am I?* Ryan asked himself.

The woman turned to him and smiled. "Hello, Ryan. I'm Mrs. Murgatroyd. I've been waiting for you. If you'd like, you can use my magical rainbow paints. You're in charge of whatever you paint. Don't panic if your picture frightens you, just paint something else."

Ryan sensed a calmness in her, a stillness against the rage boiling inside him. Quietly, Mrs. Murgatroyd placed pots of the magical paints on his table. The orange and red rainbow colors glowed, and Ryan's eyes were drawn to the red, the color of his anger. He had to do something.

He picked up a brush and dipped it into the red. He began to paint broad strokes. A slope. Two slopes, rising, meeting in a peak. A mountain. A sound like rolling thunder.

The earth trembled.

He snatched another sheet of paper, slashed with red and orange. The same mountain.

A volcano! Erupting! Paint spilled like lava in swirling rivers, pooled around the table legs, and flowed across the floor and under the door.

It *was* lava! It steamed and glowed.

Suddenly, the heat blasted the door open, blowing Ryan and his pictures out into the woods.

Now the volcano was huge. It filled the woodland — and Ryan's
school was right in the path of the fiery river! "Ha, Mark!" he shouted.
"Mrs. Jarvis! Here it comes! Serves you right!"
Everything in the lava's path burst into flames.

Deer and rabbits and raccoons raced before the fire, tails scorched.
Bushes, fences, parked cars, all flared up, engulfed by the boiling
lava. *Wait! I didn't mean for everything to burn!*

"Run, animals!" Ryan shouted.

Tongues of flame licked the school. Teachers and kids poured out
the doors, running for their lives. *There's Brandon,* Ryan thought.
*He's not so bad. He gave me one of his pet rats. And Molly! She gets
picked last for teams, too. And she loaned me the* Palooka *and* Magic Boat *videos to watch.*
The crashing rocks, the torched trees, terrified him.

Must the whole school burn down? If it did, Ryan would never get the chance to face up to Mark and his bullying, or to tell Mrs. Jarvis how he felt.

Then he remembered.

*Mrs. Murgatroyd. Didn't she say, "You're in charge of whatever you paint"? Something like that.*

The brush was in his hand. Ryan started painting again. Buttons. Control buttons. The control panel of a VCR and a gigantic TV screen.

Just as the entire school was about to go up in flames, Ryan pressed *STOP.* *REWIND.*

The river of lava flowed in reverse. The flames retreated. Trees became leafy and green again. Birds began to sing. Deer bounded backward into the woods, great chunks of rock flew in long arcs back toward the volcano, and the mountain swallowed the fire.

All was calm.

*Mrs. Murgatroyd was right! I can paint whatever I want — and I can change it if I want to. I didn't want the school to burn down, so I stopped it. I was able to make everything okay again. Better than okay! Maybe I can change things at school, too.*

Ryan thought about Mrs. Jarvis and Mark. He pressed *REWIND* again. *Hey, this is fun!*

The school came into focus. Then his classroom. The screen showed a close-up of Mrs. Jarvis. *PAUSE.*

*Now,* he thought. *Now she'll have to listen.*

"Ever since I moved and started school here," he said, "Mark and his buddies have picked on me. I know I'm not so hot at football, and the tetherball hits me more than I hit it, but I do the best I can. And when we play three flies up, or dodgeball or something, well, I might daydream a little. I might think about hitting the winning home run in the World Series or landing on Mars, or even being president someday.... "

Ryan talked and talked while Mrs. Jarvis listened.

Then he pressed *PLAY.* And Mrs. Jarvis apologized! For not listening to him before. For not really trying to understand why he was angry.

Everybody in the room was listening, paying attention — even Mark and his buddies looked impressed. Ryan felt great.

"*There* you are!" It was Miss Marlin. "We've been looking high and low for you."

Ryan blinked.

His hands were splattered with all the colors of the rainbow.

"Where's that woman?" he asked, rubbing his eyes. "There was this rainbow, see —"

"Tell it to Mrs. Jarvis. But first wash your hands," Miss Marlin said, taking him by the arm to the sink.

At lunch recess, Mark came up behind Ryan and gave him a shove. "Where do you think you're going, Rat-face?" he said.

Ryan turned around and faced Mark. "Don't call me Rat-face," he said. "And don't push me again."

"Who's gonna stop me, Rat-face?" Mark said.

Ryan stood his ground. "You really make me mad, but you're not going to get me in trouble this time. You're just a big bully."

"Ryan's right," Brandon chimed in.

"Yeah, Mark," said Molly, joining them. "Why don't you pick on somebody your own size?"

Mark looked around, but there was no one to back him up. "You wait, Rat-face," he said. "You'll be sorry."

"Oh, be quiet," said Brandon.

"Yeah," said Molly. "Why don't you get out of here, you big bully?"

Red-faced, Mark turned around and walked away without saying another word.

Ryan, Brandon, and Molly looked at each other and grinned. Ryan couldn't believe it. He had stood up to Mark without fighting and it had worked. And Brandon and Molly had stood behind him. Maybe he could talk to Mrs. Jarvis, too.

While his classmates were getting ready to go home at the end of the day, Ryan went up to his teacher. "May I talk to you in private, Mrs. Jarvis?" he asked.

"Just a minute," she said. "Class, please leave the room quietly. What is it, Ryan?"

"I want to tell you why I've been hitting and kicking kids," Ryan said, then hesitated.

"Go on," said Mrs. Jarvis. "I'm listening."

Ryan took a deep breath and began to explain as best he could. *It's just like before!* he thought. *I'm talking — and Mrs. Jarvis is listening!* With new confidence, Ryan continued.

"Mark's bigger than I am and can beat me up. Whenever he made fun of me, I'd get so mad I'd jump on anybody else who came by. But I won't do that anymore. From now on I'm going to stand up for myself — to Mark."

"It's okay to feel angry," said Mrs. Jarvis, "but bad behavior will not be tolerated." Then she smiled. "I am sorry that I didn't see what was really going on, and I'm glad you decided to talk to me."

Smiling broadly, Ryan came through the school doors. As he got in line for the bus, Molly turned around and smiled back at him. In front of her, Brandon's face bloomed into a grin, his freckles glowing reddish-brown, his eyes incredibly blue.

For a moment, Ryan was reminded of Mrs. Murgatroyd. He looked up at the sky just as the sun broke through the clouds. In the distance he saw the arc of a rainbow, fully alive, all its colors shining.